I Runned Away to Sea

Susan Gates

Illustrated by Martin Remphrey

OXFORD

UNIVERSITY PRESS

OXFORD
UNIVERSITY PRESS

Great Clarendon Street, Oxford OX2 6DP

Oxford University Press is a department of the University of Oxford.
It furthers the University's objective of excellence in research, scholarship,
and education by publishing worldwide in

Oxford   New York

Auckland   Cape Town   Dar es Salaam   Hong Kong   Karachi
Kuala Lumpur   Madrid   Melbourne   Mexico City   Nairobi
New Delhi   Shanghai   Taipei   Toronto

With offices in

Argentina   Austria   Brazil   Chile   Czech Republic   France   Greece
Guatemala   Hungary   Italy   Japan   Poland   Portugal   Singapore
South Korea   Switzerland   Thailand   Turkey   Ukraine   Vietnam

Oxford is a registered trade mark of Oxford University Press
in the UK and in certain other countries

British Library Cataloguing in Publication Data

Data available

ISBN-13: 978 0 19 919 658 6
ISBN-10: 0 19 919 658 3

7 9 10 8 6

Mixed Pack (1 of 6 different titles): ISBN-13: 978 0 19 919662 3; ISBN-10: 0 19 919662 1
Class Pack (6 copies of 6 titles): ISBN-13: 978 0 19 919661 6; ISBN-10: 0 19 919661 3

Illustrated by Martin Remphrey

Acknowledgements
p4 Aerofilms; p4/5 Corel; p5 Aerofilms; p14 Hulton-Deutsch
Collection/Corbis UK Ltd.; p18 Grimsby Telegraph; p38 Grimsby
Telegraph; p39 Francis Frith Collection; p54 Roy Starkey
postcard collection/Grimsby Telegraph; p63 Francis Frith
Collection; p92 National Maritime Museum; p92/93 Corel;
p93 Bettmann/Corbis UK Ltd.; p94/95 Corel;
p95 Grimsby Telegraph

Printed in China by Imago

Contents

Introduction

Grimsby is a well-known town on the wide mouth of the River Humber. It was once known as a major fishing port.

Goods were carried up and down the river by barge to and from the port.

Times were hard for many poor families and sometimes young boys were tempted away to seek their fortune.

Grimsby, The Docks, aerial view, 1925

This is the story of one such boy, Walter Claridge. It is set in mid-Victorian times, and whilst the characters are fictional, the setting and events surrounding them are representative of actual experiences.

Grimsby, The Docks, aerial view, 1997. What features can you recognise from the earlier photo?

1

Crows Don't Know
It's Sunday

A voice came out of the darkness. "Come on, my lad! Move your lazy bones!"

Walter Claridge snuggled down. "Oh Ma," he begged, "just two minutes more."

Someone shook his shoulder roughly.

"Get up! Else that farmer'll be after you!"

"I'm tired, Ma!"

Walter was eleven years old. From dawn until dusk he worked for a farmer, scaring crows. He didn't even have Sunday off. Because, as the farmer said, "Crows don't know it's Sunday."

"That farmer has a big stick," Ma reminded him. "And a short temper."

"I'm coming Ma!" Walter threw off the sacks that covered him. He staggered up, shivering.

"Pa's up and gone," Ma warned Walter.

Pa worked as a farm labourer for the same farmer.

"I'd best be off too!" said Walter, scared.

He pulled on his boots. They were too big. But Walter felt proud to have boots at all. They were hand-me-downs from the farmer's son. Before Walter got them, he had to spend all day out in the fields with bare feet.

"Sometimes me toes went blue!" he thought, as he pulled on his boots and snatched the grub Ma gave him. It was always the same – a bit of bread and an onion.

"Bye, Ma!" He rushed outside, into the misty dawn.

He stumbled along the muddy track. He was heading for the big field, down by the river.

His heart beat suddenly faster. Was that the farmer, high up on his horse, above the hedge?

It wasn't the farmer, come to beat him for being late. It was just a crooked tree. "You lucky lad!" Walter told himself.

Walter climbed the gate into the field. The crows were already gathering to eat the seeds.

"You thieving creatures!" Walter shouted. He hated crows.

He ran at them, waving his arms like windmills. "*Raaaa!*"

They flew off in a black cloud, their wings clattering.

Much later, when the sun was high in the sky, Walter sat down for five minutes. Chasing crows had worn him out.

Munching his onion, he stared at the river. It was a wide, grey river, running down to the sea. Walter had never seen the sea. But he'd often day-dreamed about a sailor's life.

"There are pirates!" he told himself. "And treasure islands!"

He might make his fortune. He could see himself, coming back in fine clothes, instead of the rags he was wearing now.

"I shall bring Ma back a gold brooch," he thought. "She shall have servants!"

A voice broke into his fantasies.

"Now then, you look like a lively lad!"

Walter almost jumped out of his skin. He stared up, dazzled by the sun.

But it was only the **bargee**.

"Phew!" said Walter. "You scared me, Mister."

But Walter was pleased to see him. It was lonely all by himself in the field. Sometimes he went all day without hearing a human voice. And the bargee had wonderful tales to tell. Seafaring tales, of a sailor's adventures.

The bargee had sailed on all sorts of boats – **fishing smacks**, merchant ships – he had been to China! But now he sailed a big barge up and down the River Humber. It brought manure for the farms from the hundreds of horses in the town. And went back down river, loaded with hay, to feed those same horses.

"Muck up, hay down. That's me!" the bargee always said.

"I never saw you come," said Walter.

Was he going up with muck? Or down with hay? Walter sniffed. There was no manure stink in the air. Only the sweet smell of hay.

"I'm on my way down to Grimsby," said

the bargee. "But I stopped off here, especially to see you."

The bargee was a friendly man. He had very blue, twinkling eyes.

"Budge up," said the bargee. And he sat down under the hedge, beside Walter.

"Fancy a bite to eat?" said the bargee. He took some cold bacon out of a cloth. It was a long time since Walter had tasted bacon.

He gobbled it down gratefully.

"Now if you was a fisher lad," said the bargee. "You'd never go hungry. Fisher lads get handsome victuals. And meat and pudding every day!"

"I'd think that I was in heaven!" said Walter, his eyes shining.

"But there's more," said the bargee, his merry eyes twinkling. "I'm speaking of the comradeship of the sea! All the mates you'd have and the fine times. Dancing the hornpipe and singing sea songs. Why, it's a regular holiday!"

Walter stared out at the cold, empty fields, the cawing crows. A full belly and a fine time? He could hardly imagine it.

"But aren't there storms out at sea?" he asked. "I heard there were storms. And ships got wrecked."

The bargee laughed. "Storms? Cast yer eyes on that river. Do you see any storms? Any wrecks of ships?"

Walter looked. The river seemed calm and peaceful. It rolled sluggishly along.

Sometimes the wind whipped it into quite big waves.

"But I am not afraid of that," reasoned Walter. "So why should I be afraid of the sea?"

He was beginning to get really excited. He'd often dreamed of it. But dare he do it? Dare he run away to sea?

As if he was reading Walter's mind, the bargee said, in a coaxing voice, "Just step onto my barge. I shall take you straight to Grimsby, where merry times are waiting."

"I shall do it!" said Walter, suddenly springing up. " But first I have to tell Ma."

"Better not!" said the bargee, rather too quickly. "You can write to her from Grimsby. And think what she will say when you come home rich, dressed in fine clothes, with all those gold coins jingling in your pocket!"

"Take me to Grimsby then!" cried Walter, starry-eyed.

Now he'd decided, he couldn't wait to escape. To leave behind these muddy fields and the long, dreary hours he'd spent crouching in them, freezing cold and lonely.

The bargee put his arm round Walter's skinny shoulders. "There's my fine, strong lad!" he told him. "You made a brave choice. You won't regret it."

"*Caw, caw!*" came the mocking cry of the crows.

"Hurry, boy," said the bargee. Looking over his shoulder to check no one was watching, he hustled Walter down to the river bank and aboard the barge.

The last Thames sailing barge, the Cambria, sails up the river to Tower Pier

2

Greener than a Cabbage

"I should have runned away to sea before!" thought Walter. "That bargee was right. It's a fine life!"

Far better than scaring crows. The barge drifted down the river like a floating haystack. The day was bright and golden.

Walter stretched out on the soft hay and watched the fields slide by.

He was too excited to feel much guilt. There was just a little pang when he thought of Ma.

"She will have fits," he thought, "when I don't come home from the fields. She will weep her eyes out."

But then he thought, "I shall send her a letter as soon as I reach Grimsby." That made him feel much better. "And soon I shall be home for my first holidays."

The bargee had told him that fisher lads had many holidays. Why they hardly worked at all! And when they did, they earned a small fortune. Two pounds a week. And to think that that stingy farmer paid him four pennies for scaring crows!

Walter couldn't wait to start his new life.

"I shall see the world," he murmured to himself happily, snuggling down in the warm hay. "I shall have adventures."

He must have dozed off.

"Right, boy!"

It was the bargee shaking him. His eyes didn't seem as twinkling as before, nor his smile as merry. "We have some business to settle, you and I."

Walter stared wide-eyed around him. Where was he? He was still groggy with sleep. He saw fishing masts, a whole forest of them, and grey water and screeching gulls. And on the dockside, crowds of people, carts and horses.

"Is this Grimsby?" he asked, amazed. He picked some hay out of his hair.

"Make haste now," said the bargee. "You'll have to be sharper than that when you're at sea."

Walter followed him down the wobbling plank from the barge to the dockside.

"Is that the sea?" asked Walter, his eyes filled with wonder. Beyond the dock gates, grey, glittering water stretched to the horizon. It was as smooth as their village pond, just as the bargee had promised.

"The sea?" laughed the bargee. " No, bless you, boy, that's still the river. You'll see the

Grimsby Dock Tower as seen from the Royal Docks. This view of The Docks is very much the one that Walter would have seen

open sea soon enough."

Then he was gone. Walter raced after him, afraid of being left behind. He dodged people, horses. He scurried down stinking streets, crammed with tiny houses. The noise, the jostling crowds, made his head spin. Women were screeching, drunk seamen roaring. Everywhere was the stench of rotting fish. It filled your nostrils, made your eyes water.

Someone plucked at his coat from a dark doorway, "Another fisher lad fresh from the country! Come here fisher lad!"

Walter tore away and ended up panting beside the bargee, in front of a grand, red brick building.

"This is where I hands you over," said the bargee.

Another man appeared out of nowhere. "I never knowed such an innocent as this one," whispered the bargee to him. "He's greener than a cabbage!"

The other man had a black beard and a thin, lined face. His eyes weren't like the bargee's. They were hard and unsmiling. He looked Walter up and down. "He's skinny as a rabbit," was all he said.

"But he's keen as mustard," said the bargee.

Walter nodded eagerly. "I so want to go to sea, Sir. It's been what I dreamed of. The

bargee told me such tales!"

"*Humph*," said the other man. He didn't seem impressed.

There were some more whispered words between him and the bargee. Walter saw some silver coins counted out. Then, clasping his money, the bargee plunged back into the crowds.

"You shall have your new clothes," said the stern, bearded man, "after you have signed a piece of paper."

"New clothes?" marvelled Walter. He looked down at his own rags. His jacket was thin and full of holes. When he was crow scaring, the wind whistled through it. "I did not know I would get new clothes straight away!"

Inside the grand building, another man, white haired and impatient, sat at a high desk. He fired questions at Walter. "When were you born, lad? In what place? Speak up! I haven't got all day. I have a dozen more **indentures** to make out."

Walter stumbled over the answers. All this

hurry made him tongue-tied.

He had no idea where he was, or why he was here. And he didn't dare ask. While the man at the desk wrote busily, Walter thought about those new clothes.

"Will I get boots?" he wondered. "Will they be brand new?"

He had never, in his life, had a pair of brand new boots. How his brothers' eyes would pop, when he went back home to see them.

That reminded him. "I must write to Ma," he thought. "And tell her that I runned away to sea. But that I am all right. And not to worry her head about me."

"Put your name here," said the man at the desk. He pushed a large sheet of paper, covered with writing, towards Walter. Obediently, Walter scrawled, "Walter Claridge".

The man at the desk asked the stern man. "Are you sure the lad ain't stupid, **Skipper**? He doesn't speak up well. He hardly seems to know his own name."

"At least he can write it," the Skipper scowled. "Not like those other workhouse scum and beggar boys that the bargee found for me."

"I am your **Master** now," the Skipper said to Walter. "I am owner of the fishing smack *Mary Anne*. And you have signed yourself on as my **apprentice**. For ten years."

"Ten years?" thought Walter. He stopped thinking about new boots. For the first time he felt a tiny twist of doubt. Ten years seemed like an eternity.

"But I am sure I shall like being an apprentice," Walter told himself. "So ten years will pass by in a flash."

With his new Master leading the way, they dived back into the teeming streets. Walter skidded on fish scales and fish guts.

"Watch out, lad!"

A stamping horse, all steaming from hauling a fish cart, had almost flattened him.

"You'll have to be sharper than that when you're at sea," said his new Master, the Skipper of the *Mary Anne*.

"The bargee told me that too," thought Walter, puzzled. "Why do folk keep saying that to me? And where are my new clothes that I was promised?"

The Skipper stopped abruptly, "Here's your lodgings, boy. Be on board the *Mary Anne* tomorrow by first light. Work hard, follow orders and you'll have nothing to worry about."

He went striding off, shoving his way down the busy street. Walter stared after him. His brain was whirling. What was he meant to do now?

The house where his master had abandoned him had a dusty front garden. There were fishermen's **oilskins** drying over straggly bushes and sea boots lined up by the door.

"I think you're meant to go in," Walter told himself. He swallowed hard twice. Then walked up the path.

He knocked. Did someone call "Come in"?

He yanked open the door, tripped over the step and fell inside.

Instantly, he was trapped in some kind of snare. Ropes tightened round his head and body. "Help! Help!" he shouted. He kicked out but only got more tangled.

"Be still, boy!" hissed a voice, right in his ear. "Stop struggling. Or three days' work will be ruined!"

3

An Incorrigible Boy

Walter stared around him. He had never been in such a strange place. Fishing nets hung everywhere. Across the door, the windows. The whole room seemed made of nets.

"It's how I make my living," Mrs Kettle, his

landlady, explained, after she had freed him.

"A poor widow lady must do something to put food in her mouth. I takes in apprentices. And I makes fishing nets."

Mrs Kettle was the sister of the Skipper of the *Mary Anne*. She had the same thin face. Her hair was scraped back in a bun. She was a glum lady, with a red, sniffling nose and watery eyes.

"I am all alone in the world," she told Walter, blowing her nose noisily. "My husband was drowned at sea."

"Drowned?" said Walter.

"Don't sound so surprised," said Mrs Kettle, grimly. "The sea takes many good men – and fisher lads too."

"She is just trying to frighten me," decided Walter. She trudged before him up the narrow stairs, her black dress rustling.

"This is your bedroom," she said, opening a door. Walter saw two iron beds, a wonky table.

"At least you seem like a quiet lad," she said, gloomily. "Not like that other apprentice. He has a cunning look in his eye. And far too much cheek for my liking." Walter heard her sniffling all the way down the stairs.

"What other apprentice?" wondered Walter.

The bedroom door crashed open.

A tall, bony boy burst into the room. "Are you bound for sea on the good ship *Mary*

Anne?" He stuck out his hand. "Alfred's the name. Pleased to meet ya!"

The other apprentice was a bold, swaggering lad. Walter could see at once that he wasn't a shy country boy.

He was dressed in a blue jacket with a velvet collar. "That is a fine jacket," said Walter.

"This," said Alfred glancing down at

himself. "It's better than the rags I come here in. It was give me by the Master. It's shore clothes for us apprentices. For sea you get oilskins and sea boots and two pairs of good, thick socks if you're lucky."

"Socks?" said Walter, his eyes wide with wonder. He'd never had one pair of socks, let alone two. This boy seemed to know all about a fisher lad's life. "You must have been to sea lots of times," said Walter.

"Never clapped eyes on the sea," said Alfred cheerily. "It's my first trip out tomorrow, just like you. But I'm not bothered. It can't be no worse than that workhouse I was in."

"Weren't you afraid", said Walter, "that you would get lost in the streets of Grimsby? What crowds of people!"

"Crowds?" grinned Alfred. "I can see you ain't a city boy. Why, this is nothing compared to London."

"London!" said Walter, deeply impressed. "You have come here all the way from London?"

"I was sent here to be a fisher lad," said Alfred. "It was just to get rid of me. Them workhouse guardians said I was incorrigible. That means they couldn't do nothing with me."

Alfred sprawled on his iron bed. "These lodgings ain't bad," he said. "You get bacon and cabbage for dinner. But Ma Kettle is a gloomy old bird. Always going on about the sea taking many good men."

"She said that to me!" laughed Walter. "She's just trying to scare us."

"Well, she won't scare me," said Alfred. "I'm a London lad. I know a thing or two. Stick with me", he told Walter, "and you'll be all right."

"I will," said Walter gratefully. Since his new friend seemed so worldly-wise, Walter asked him another question. "Do you think Mrs Kettle might give me paper? I want to write to my Ma."

"No use asking *me* about letters," said Alfred. "I never learned to read nor write."

With his belly full of cabbage and bacon,

Walter lay in his iron bed. He was only covered by a rough, scratchy blanket. But it wasn't the cold that kept him awake. It was excitement.

"I hardly feel worried at all," he thought, surprised. "Yet I have started a brand new life!"

Only this morning he was a crow scarer, freezing his toes off in a field. But, tomorrow, he was going to sea as a fisher lad on the *Mary Anne*.

The moon came out from a cloud and washed the room with silver. Walter looked proudly at his new clothes. The master had sent them round to Mrs Kettle's. There were shore clothes, just like Alfred's. And for going to sea tomorrow, sea boots, socks, trousers, oilskins and two big, thick **guernseys**.

"Alfred?" said Walter to the shadowy lump in the other bed. "Are you asleep?"

At first there was no answer. "I knew he wouldn't be lying awake like me," thought Walter. Alfred was fourteen years old and came from London. "He's not scared of anything," thought Walter.

But then suddenly Alfred whispered, "Do you think they beat you out at sea?"

"Beat you?" repeated Walter. "I don't know. The farmer sometimes beat me. When I fell asleep in the field."

"Well, I was beat something shocking by my Dad," said Alfred. " And all for nothing! When he got drunk, he would beat us with a broom handle. That's before he left and we ended up in the workhouse. I got beat there too. So, you see, I just couldn't stand any more of it."

Walter frowned. He couldn't think what to say. Then he remembered the Master's words. "If we work hard," he told Alfred, "and follow orders, we will have nothing to worry about."

"I ain't worried!" said Alfred, defensively.

There was one thing, though, that still worried Walter. "Alfred," he said. "Does your Ma know you're here?"

"My Ma died," said Alfred, "in the workhouse of a fever. Else I would have sent her a letter. Except I can't write."

Alfred pulled the blanket up over his head. He didn't want Walter to hear him sobbing. He was supposed to be tough, an incorrigible boy, who never cried about anything.

Drowned, in the Blink of an Eye

Someone shook Walter awake.

"I'm tired, Ma!" he moaned, turning over.

Then he realised. It wasn't Ma, it was Mrs Kettle, getting Alfred and him out of bed for their first trip out on the *Mary Anne*.

Alfred poked a tatty head out of the covers. "It's still dark!" he groaned.

"The tide waits for no man, nor fisher lad neither," said Mrs Kettle, rustling out of the room in her black frock.

The tiny bedroom was like ice, even colder than their cottage. But this time, Walter had warm clothes to pull on, and sea boots.

Downstairs, Mrs Kettle said, "No time for breakfast." She shoved some cold meat into their hands.

"Hey," said Alfred to Mrs Kettle, "Walter's socks has got holes in them. They're not new!"

"I expect they was some other apprentice's before they was his," said Mrs Kettle gloomily. "Maybe the last one on the *Mary Anne*, what fell from the mast. He was drowned, in the blink of an eye."

Walter shivered. Was he really wearing a dead boy's socks? Or was it just Ma Kettle telling her usual horror stories.

Mrs Kettle had one last warning. "I'd keep that mouth buttoned if I was you," she told Alfred. "The crew don't like a lad with too much lip."

Walter forgot about the dead boy's socks as they hurried through the dark streets down to the docks. His new sea boots felt clumpy. But he didn't mind. Other men and apprentices in sea boots were rushing down to catch the tide, yawning, wolfing down their breakfasts.

"I'm a proper fisher lad now," thought Walter, proudly. Soon he would be part of the ship's jolly crew. What had the bargee said about the comradeship of the sea?

Another fisher boy, only half awake, staggered into him.

"Sorry," said Walter, smiling.

"Oh, go hang yourself," snarled the other boy, as he dived down a stinking back alley.

It was barely dawn but the docks were bustling. In the grey light, Walter saw fishing smacks, their white sails hoisted, gliding out to sea.

"How will we find the *Mary Anne*?" he asked Alfred anxiously.

"She is down in the Royal Dock. This way," said Alfred.

Grimsby trawler fishermen

"You know everything!" said Walter, amazed. "You must have been to sea before."

"I told you, I never even seen it! But I makes it my business to know things," said Alfred, tapping the side of his nose. "It's how you get by in London."

Walter thanked his lucky stars that Alfred was on the same ship as he was. "Stick with

Alfred," he told himself. "And you'll be all right."

There was no cheery greeting when they found the *Mary Anne*, moored at the dock-side among the other fishing smacks. The Master was wearing a bowler hat to show he was Skipper. His thin, bony face didn't look pleased to see them.

Grimsby, The Docks, 1893

"Climb aboard," he said, sharply. "And keep out of the way of the **first mate** when he's working."

The deck of the *Mary Anne* looked to Walter like a muddle of ropes, sails, nets and fish baskets. But the first mate moved about, hauling on ropes, unfurling sails. He seemed to know exactly what he was doing.

He didn't smile either. Just threw them a scornful glance.

"Get below," he said. "Until we clear the dock gates. I don't want to be tripping over you."

"His socks has got holes in them," said Alfred, jerking his thumb at Walter. "He should have new ones."

Over Alfred's head, the mate and the Skipper shot a surprised look at each other. That look said, "We'll have to keep an eye on this one."

The cabin was tiny, with four bunks, a table, and a rusty iron stove. It stank of rotting fish and tobacco. As Walter and Alfred huddled side by side on a bunk they felt the *Mary Anne* move.

"We're going out to sea!" whispered Walter.

He was thrilled but his stomach felt full of wild, beating wings. He wanted to be a good fisher lad and follow orders. But this boat wasn't like the floating haystack. Walter didn't know the names of half of the things he'd seen on deck. Much less what to do with them.

"I'm a bit worried now," admitted Walter.

"I'm not!" said Alfred, in his chirpiest voice. "I been in worse places than at sea." He clamped his hands under his armpits to stop them shaking.

The *Mary Anne* had been gliding smoothly. Suddenly, she gave a shudder and a big lurch.

"*Yurgh!*" Walter clutched his stomach. Was he going to be sick? The *Mary Anne* was rocking wildly. What was happening out there?

The Skipper ducked down into the cabin. "Get some sea water, boy," he said to Alfred. He pointed to a coil of rope and a wooden

bucket by the stove. "Then both of you scrub the deck."

"Mind that **undertow**," the Skipper called after them.

"What's he mean?" thought Walter. But he didn't dare ask.

On deck, Walter blinked spray from his eyes. A howling wind whipped his hair. The *Mary Anne* was flying through huge, green waves. They seemed high as mountains! Foamy sea water crashed over her, then slid off the decks, then crashed again.

Alfred staggered into him as the *Mary Anne* tipped up, then down, up, then down.

"This is the open sea!" screamed Walter skidding down the deck. He grabbed the mast to save himself. Where was the first mate? He'd been at the tiller but now he was below decks with the Master.

"Fill the bucket!" he shrieked at Albert. Sea water was streaming down his face. He was already soaked through. The *Mary Anne* gave a sickening lurch.

Albert steadied himself on the heaving

deck. He was staring, eyes wide with horror, at the churning, green waves.

"I never thought the sea would be like this!"

"Fill the bucket!" Walter yelled, still clutching the mast. "Alfred!"

But Alfred seemed in a trance. One end of the rope was tied to the bucket handle. He twisted the other end round both wrists. Then he hurled the wooden bucket overboard into the sea.

"Walter!"

Alfred was trying to haul the bucket in. The sea wouldn't let him. Frantically, he tried to loose the wet rope around his wrists. It only gripped tighter. In seconds, Alfred was yanked shrieking overboard. The sea swallowed him whole.

The *Mary Anne* went flying on and left him far behind.

Walter stared at the empty space on deck where his friend had just been. Spray beat into his face. At first, he was too shocked even to cry out. Then something clicked inside his head. He screamed, "Help. Help. Alfred's fallen in! Stop the ship!"

The Skipper came up on deck. The first mate didn't bother.

The Skipper stared overboard and shook his head. " Drowned and we're hardly clear of the lock gates! He didn't heed what I said about the undertow!"

The Skipper shook his head. He seemed more angry than sad. "I knew that boy weren't suited to a life at sea."

After Alfred drowned, Walter's first sea trip became a nightmare. For hours, he crouched miserably in the cabin, crying. Then the Skipper and first mate lost patience. "Get a grip on yourself, lad. You're here to work!"

But Walter was dazed by shock. The orders they yelled at him didn't make sense. "Pay out the **trawl warp**!" "Lower the **leads**!" They tried to teach him, but his mind couldn't take it in. He stumbled about, soaking wet, freezing cold. Every heave of the *Mary Anne* made him sick. He cut his hands hauling ropes and the salt water stung in the open wounds.

"Make some tea!" yelled the first mate. "That's all you're good for!"

But he couldn't do it fast enough so the first mate cuffed him.

They were hauling in a net full of wriggling, silver fish. But Walter's sore cracked hands wouldn't hold it. It slipped back into the sea. For that the Skipper lashed a rope's end across his face, cutting it to the bone.

"You dozy boy! Don't stand there daydreaming!"

But Walter wasn't daydreaming. He was grieving for his friend, Alfred, who had drowned, like Mrs Kettle said, in the blink of an eye.

There was never any peace. The noise never stopped. Every second of the day and night, the wind screamed and the deep green sea battered the *Mary Anne,* as if it wanted to smash her to bits.

CHAPTER

Running Away *From* Sea

Three days after Alfred drowned, the *Mary Anne* sailed from the open sea back into the calm, grey water of Grimsby dock.

Walter stood on deck. He hadn't been away long but it felt like a lifetime. The dock hadn't changed. It was as crammed with ships, as busy and lively as ever.

But Walter had changed. A different boy sailed into harbour from the one who had gone out to sea. He was bruised from the first mate's fists and cut from the rope's end. Going out, he'd been smiling, excited. But now his face looked as stony and grim as the Skipper's.

The *Mary Anne* moored by the dockside. Walter couldn't help himself. He started to climb off the boat on to dry land.

A rough hand grabbed his shoulder. "Where do you think you're going, boy? There's the catch to unload."

"I don't like the sea!" Walter blurted out desperately. "I wanted to go to sea once. But I don't want to go no more!"

The Skipper said, "What are you babbling about, boy? You're a poor fisher lad. But you're better than nothing. And you're my apprentice now. All signed and legal. You try to run and I'll send the police after you. You'll end up in Lincoln prison."

"Prison?" thought Walter. He didn't understand. "But I thought I could go home if I didn't like it."

The Skipper laughed. Walter had never seen him laugh before. "The bargee was right, boy. You're greener than a cabbage. Just be here, day after tomorrow. Mrs Kettle will tell you when. And don't make the ship wait."

"Don't I get no money?" Walter dared to ask.

"Money?" said the Skipper. He was scowling now. "I'm teaching you a trade. I'm paying your lodgings. You may get a few pence pocket money. If I feels like giving it to you. And I don't, at present."

Walter trailed back to Ma Kettle's through the smelly, swarming streets. His hair was crusty with sea salt and his boots soggy with water. They felt heavy as lead. He was on dry land but he could still feel the bucking of the *Mary Anne*. He was suddenly sick in a doorway.

It seemed to clear his mind a bit. "I ain't going back," he decided. "Even if I get put in

prison. I ain't going back."

But how was he going to escape? He'd already worked out that Ma Kettle was a spy for the Master. If she saw him running he'd be captured in no time.

"Be clever," he told himself. "What would Alfred do?"

He didn't knock at the front door of his lodgings. He stayed in the garden, sneaked behind a gooseberry bush, and waited.

After a long time, Ma Kettle came out with a basket. She was wearing a black bonnet and shawl. She was going shopping. She locked her front door.

When she was out of sight, Alfred crept round the back of the house. It wasn't hard to find a way in. He just pushed up a rotten window frame.

"Mind the fishing net," Walter warned himself, climbing in.

This time he didn't get tangled up.

He hurried up to his bedroom. He didn't intend to be here long. Just long enough to change his sea clothes.

He felt a sharp pain twisting inside him. He'd just seen Alfred's shore clothes stacked on his bed. But he didn't cry.

"I'm going to escape, Alfred," he told the pile of clothes. "I'm running away *from* the sea."

He put on his own shore clothes, the blue trousers and blue jacket with a velvet collar. He took off the sea boots he'd been so proud of and pulled on his old, crow scaring boots.

"Better make haste," he told himself nervously. "Before old Ma Kettle comes back."

On his way out, he hesitated. He was hungry. He snatched some bread from the pantry, just a small crust. Ma Kettle would never miss it,

And then he was outside the house. Hurrying through streets, keeping close to walls, dodging down alley ways. He kept checking over his shoulder. He never saw Ma Kettle or the first mate or his Master. But what was that? He spied tall, hard hats and brass buttons shining.

"Policemen!" he thought, panicking.

There were two of them, walking side by side, as they always did in the rough parts of town.

In this picture taken in about 1906, the two policemen are standing in Riby Square, Grimsby. This is before the days of traffic lights, so they are directing any traffic flow

His heart thumping, he cowered in a stinking alleyway. Was it safe to go out? He daren't look. But then a drunken seaman barged into him. "Want a fight?"

Walter shot out of the alleyway. He thought he was running straight into the arms of the policemen. But they were nowhere in sight.

At last the houses ran out and he reached the fields. He breathed a sigh of relief. He was free! And he even had a plan. His plan was to find the River Humber. He could already see it, glinting in the distance. Then all he had to do was follow it back home.

He walked all day along the river banks. He didn't think about anything much. Except how pleased his Ma would be to see him.

"You never wrote her that letter," he scolded himself. "She will be worried sick."

When he'd finished the bread he nibbled whatever he could find. Turnips from the field and sweet chestnuts from a tree. He wished Alfred was with him.

"I could have showed him how to catch a

rabbit. I bet he never did that, being a city boy."

But thinking about Alfred made him too sad, so he whistled to try and cheer himself up.

Every time he looked at the Humber flowing smoothly by, the same thought mocked him: "You thought the sea was like that! They was right. You was innocent as a baby ."

He gave a bitter smile. Well, he was different now. He was wiser and although he'd only been gone four days, he felt years older.

Then it grew dark and he was too weary to walk any further. He crept under a hedge, curled up like a squirrel and slept...

Walter's eyes shot open. At first, he was dazzled by sunlight. Then he saw a fat, red, angry face poking straight into his.

Someone dragged him out from under the bush. A voice thundered at him.

"An escaped fisher lad, I see by your clothes! Trespassing in my field! And stealing my turnips I'll be bound. You come along with me! It's the police station for you, you young rogue!"

CHAPTER

No Better than Slavery

Walter had handcuffs on his wrists. He was chained to the boys on either side of him. They were in a carriage on a slow, rattling train. The other two prisoners were fisher lads too. They were bound, like Walter, for Lincoln Jail.

The fisher lad on Walter's right fidgeted. He was even younger and smaller than Walter. He had a sad, creased face like a sick baby monkey. Clink! His chain clattered.

"Stow that racket!" warned the policeman sitting opposite them.

"Sorry, Sir," the sickly lad squeaked. He put his head down and stared at his chained hands.

There was no one else in the carriage with them. At Grimsby, some ladies had looked in. They wrinkled their noses in disgust, then moved on. Respectable ladies don't want to ride with criminals.

Walter stared out of the train window. They were trundling through grey, rainy fields. Billows of black smoke drifted back from the engine. Mixed with the sooty smell was a familiar fishy stink. The train was carrying fresh fish, packed in ice, to be sold in Lincoln.

This was Walter's first ever train ride. He should have been bouncing about with excitement. But he was too worried about what was waiting when he got to his journey's end.

Besides, even the tiniest movement made his chains clank.

The policeman yawned. He scratched himself. He yawned again. The swaying of the train and the stuffy carriage had made him sleepy. Slowly, his head fell on to his chest. After a few seconds, he began to snore.

"*Psst!*"

The sickly lad was tugging at Walter's sleeve. His chain clinked like mad. "*Shhh!*" said Walter. But the policeman didn't wake up.

"We could escape!" whispered the sickly boy. "Throw ourselves off the train and make a run for it."

The boy on Walter's left was big and strong and slow-speaking. "Why?" he said. "They'd only catch us and send us back to sea. I'd rather be in prison."

"Have you been in prison?" hissed Walter.

"Loads of times," shrugged the slow-speaking boy. "For disobeying orders mostly. Me and the second mate didn't get on."

"Well, I ain't going back to sea!" said the sickly boy, shuddering. "The **deck hand** said, 'You filthy lad. You've got lice!' He made me eat some. Then I got towed behind the ship to wash me! I was nearly drowned!"

He dived towards the carriage door. "I'm going to jump!"

"You'll get crushed under the wheels," said

the slow-speaking boy in a matter-of-fact way.

"I don't care. I'd rather be dead than go back to sea. I cannot stand it!"

"*Ow!*" He gave a yelp of pain. A blue-sleeved arm had grabbed his shoulder, forced him back into his seat. The policeman was wide awake. "Don't give me no trouble, boy. Behave yourself! We're nearly there."

The sickly boy's body was suddenly racked by coughing.

"If he escaped," thought Walter, "he wouldn't get far in that state."

Walter stared out of the train window. Suddenly a cry of amazement burst from his mouth. "*Woooo!* What's that place?"

The building soared into the sky, all spires and stained glass windows. It towered above the town. The houses clustered beneath it like doll's house furniture.

The policeman didn't cry, "Silence boy!" After his nap he was in a better mood.

"Why, boy," he answered, "don't you know nothing? That's Lincoln Cathedral. And next

Lincoln Cathedral in 1890.
Next to the cathedral is Lincoln
prison, although you can't see
it here, and Walter doesn't see
it at first. He is overcome by
the splendour of the cathedral
building

to it is Lincoln Castle. Where you lot will be locked up."

Walter stopped staring at the cathedral. He shifted his gaze to the grim castle walls. An icy hand seemed to squeeze his heart.

Locked up! He still couldn't believe it. After the farmer had found him everything had been a blur. He'd been hauled up before the magistrates, stern men in black robes. He'd been sentenced to ten days' jail. For running away from sea and for stealing a turnip.

A magistrate said, "We will be lenient because it is the boy's first offence."

Even if he got the chance, Walter wasn't sure now whether to write that letter to Ma. "She'll die of shame," he thought.

It was a long, steep climb to the castle. People stopped to stare at the fisher lads, clanking in chains along the main street. Some shrank away, one spat. But many eyes were shocked and full of pity.

"Buy my fine, fresh flowers!" someone was shouting. A girl with red hair was selling violets from a tray. She dashed forward and stuck a flower into Walter's jacket.

"You poor fisher lads. It's no better than slavery!" she cried out.

"Slavery? Is she talking about me?" thought Walter, bewildered.

"Back off there," growled the policeman to the flower seller, his hand going to the wooden stick he wore hanging from his belt.

The three prisoners shuffled on, with the policeman puffing beside them. The sickly lad was coughing worse than ever. He had to stop and rest.

"Me chest hurts!" he told the policeman. "And I keeps coughing up blood."

"Don't tell me," said the policeman. "I ain't your mother."

At the top of the hill, Walter looked up. His mouth fell open. His eyes travelled up to the very top spires of Lincoln Cathedral. He had never seen anything so wonderful. It stole your breath away.

The policeman yanked at his chain. "Make haste, boy. You've no time to stare at cathedrals. Prison is where you're heading."

They trudged in behind him through the great stone gate and heard doors clang shut behind them.

7

A Whole Spoon of Treacle

There was nothing in Walter's prison cell but a bed, a chair and a wooden shelf with a Bible on it. Through the bars of his tiny window he could see clouds and blue sky.

He waited, his heart fluttering, for something to happen. Nothing did. He was left alone, staring at the bare brick walls.

"Prison is a miserable place for a boy to be," thought Walter.

But at least they'd taken the chains off. And left him in peace. There were no shrieking winds, no crashing waves. No one screaming orders that didn't make sense.

Then the keys jangled in his cell door.

Scared, Walter looked up. But it was only the chaplain, swooping in like a big, black bat, his robes fluttering.

"Boy! I hope you are thinking about your crimes," said the chaplain sternly. "And how you have brought shame on your parents."

"My parents don't know I am here!" Walter burst out.

"Do not *know*? You must write and inform them immediately," said the chaplain.

Walter was given ink and paper. He bit his lip. What was he going to write? He'd been gone barely a week, yet so much had happened. He couldn't squeeze it all into one letter. In the end, he wrote:

Dear Ma and Pa,

I runned away to sea. I am sorry for it now and sorry for not telling you. I hate the sea. I was treated worse than a slave. I am in prison now in Lincoln Castle because I runned away from my Master. Please come and save me. I promise I will be a good lad when I get out of prison but, please, I don't want to go to sea again.

Your respectful son,
Walter Claridge.

The chaplain was looking over his shoulder. He seemed to approve. "I am glad you are sorry for your crimes." He took the letter away. "I shall make sure that this is posted."

A prison guard, with bunches of jangling keys, undid Walter's cell door.

"You! Dinner time!"

Walter was let out into a line of shuffling prisoners. Some were young lads like him, some were bent and wrinkled old men. He looked out for the fisher lads he'd been chained to. There was the slow-speaking boy! He tried to signal to him.

"No communication between prisoners!" growled a guard.

Walter lowered his head again.

They sat at long tables, spooning down meat and potatoes. The slow-speaking boy was right. The grub was better in here than at sea.

Walter listened out for the coughing of the sickly lad. He didn't hear it. "I hope he hasn't died," thought Walter. "I hope he is in the prison hospital." But he never saw the boy again.

After dinner, the prisoners sat in long rows. They picked apart old tarry ropes so they could be used again to plug the gaps between the planks of wooden ships.

"Silence!" roared the guards if anyone tried to talk. "Do you want a punishment?"

Walter picked more furiously. The thought of punishment filled his mind with terror. He had heard of floggings and the treadmill where men went round and round in a wheel until they dropped.

His hands were already sore and cracked from the sea. Picking ropes apart made them bleed even more. Supper time was watery porridge, with a spoonful of treacle to sweeten it.

"A whole spoon of treacle!" thought Walter, as pleased as if he'd been given a treasure chest.

They had to eat it in total silence. He dared to glance up and saw the slow-speaking boy spooning down his grub like a hungry wolf.

Locked back in his cell, Walter stared out of his tiny window. The sky was fiery red from the setting sun.

A prison guard clattered his stick against the bars. "Get in bed, boy!"

Walter lay on his thin, straw mattress. He thought of Ma and Pa and his brothers, far away in their tiny cottage. It wasn't dark yet.

Pa would still be out in the fields. What would he be doing now? Picking stones out of the mud? Digging potatoes?

"Get my letter soon, Ma and Pa," wished Walter.

He had to do his ten days in jail. He knew Ma and Pa, who were poor people, didn't have the power to change that.

"But they've got to free me from my Master somehow," thought Walter. "They've just got to! Because I couldn't stand going to sea again."

That night he had a dreadful dream. He dreamed that he was back on the *Mary Anne*. Great, green waves towered over her, high as Lincoln Cathedral. The wind was shrieking like demons. Then, through the spray, he saw Alfred, struggling in the sea, waving and screaming for help.

"Save him, save him!" yelled Walter. "He's not drowned yet. He's still alive."

But when he turned round, it wasn't the Skipper with his hand on the tiller. It was old Ma Kettle.

"It's no use," said Ma Kettle in her gloomiest voice. "The sea will never give him up. Didn't I tell you? It takes many a good man – and fisher lad."

And, leaving Alfred behind, she steered the *Mary Anne* on into the storm.

Walter woke up sweating and terrified. Then he saw bare, brick walls around him. Heard a guard shouting, "Look, lively you lazy rogue!" And was almost pleased to find he wasn't at sea at all. But only in a prison cell.

8

Muck Up, Hay Down

Walter blinked in the sunshine. The street was crowded and noisy. There were horses, carts, people. From a doorway, the red-haired flower seller was yelling, "Buy my fine violets!"

He'd forgotten there was a world out here, just beyond the prison walls. After one day in prison he felt he'd been there for a hundred years. Every day was the same – gruel, picking ropes, dinner of meat and potatoes, picking more ropes.

Except, one day, even the guards couldn't stop the men murmuring, "He's for the drop today." Somewhere, in a cell in the prison, a man was waiting to be hanged.

But mostly, Walter tried not to listen to the talk of treadmills, floggings and executions. He closed his ears, shut his mind down, and just tried to survive.

Now his ten days was up. He'd been pushed out of the gates in his shore clothes with no money and no food. But at least he was free.

"You haven't even made a plan!" he said to himself, staring round, bewildered.

He rubbed the scar on his cheek where the Master had cut him with the rope's end. There was one thing he was sure of. He was never going back to sea.

His brain told him, "Run! Run back home!" There was nothing to stop him, was there?

And then he saw Ma Kettle, standing across the street, watching him.

She was wearing a dress, black as crows, and her gloomiest look.

She came rustling forward. "I was sent", she told Walter, "by the Master to bring you back to Grimsby. You're wanted on board the *Mary Anne*."

Walter looked wildly round. Why not just disappear in the crowds? She would never catch him, in her tight, black button-up boots.

"I shouldn't if I was you," said Ma Kettle, reading his mind. "Folk will take one look at your shore clothes and say, 'That's a fisher lad on the run.' Do you want to go back to prison?"

Walter looked behind him at the grim prison walls. He didn't want to go back in there. He didn't want to go to sea either.

"I'm trapped," he thought, desperately.

Meekly, he followed Ma Kettle to the railway station. He couldn't think of anything else to do.

She took a letter out of her big, black handbag.

"Your Ma and Pa wrote to the Master," she told Walter, "begging him to end your apprenticeship."

"I knew they would save me!" said Walter, overjoyed. "I wrote them a letter from prison saying I runned away to sea."

Mrs Kettle gave him a doom-filled look. She shook her head sadly. "Fisher lads can't escape that easy," she said. "The Master wrote back. He wrote you were his for ten years, once you'd signed that paper. And to get you freed they would have to pay him twenty pounds."

"Twenty pounds!" gasped Walter. His hopes crumbled to dust. How would his parents find twenty pounds? Ma and Pa had barely had twenty spare pence in their whole lives.

"Never mind," said Ma Kettle. In her own glum way she was trying to be kind. "There's worse things than being at sea."

"No there isn't!" screamed Walter, inside his head. "No there isn't! Look what happened to Alfred!"

As the train steamed through the flat fields, Walter didn't even look out of the window. He hung his head and stared at his hands. He wasn't in chains this time. But he felt like a prisoner, just the same.

The closer he got to Grimsby, the more helpless he felt. His parents couldn't afford to buy his freedom. With the Master, the first mate, the police, the magistrates and Ma Kettle all against him, what could one lad on his own do?

The train shuddered to a stop. The signs said, "GRIMSBY TOWN". Walter thought, "I'm here again!" There was no escape. He would have to go back to sea.

Numbed by misery, he stumbled after Ma Kettle down to the docks.

Other apprentices shoved him out of the way. Horse and cart drivers yelled, "*Oi*, there! Mind out!" But he hardly noticed.

"Now where's the *Mary Anne*?" wondered Ma Kettle, scanning the crowds of fishing smacks.

Walter lifted his eyes. They were dull and hopeless. But suddenly, they lit up with the tiniest sparkle.

He'd seen something familiar. He could

smell it too. It was the barge with the bargee who had told him all those lies. It was moored on the other side of the dock. And this time it wasn't loaded with sweet-smelling hay. It was piled up with a mountain of steaming horse manure.

"Muck up, hay down!" thought Walter. That barge was going up river. It would take him back home. It practically passed by his own front door!

His brain had almost given up. But now it started working again, furiously.

Ma Kettle had spotted the *Mary Anne*. Walter looked where she was waving. The sight of the Master in his bowler hat gave him a chill of horror. Had the Master seen him yet?

"I don't think so," thought Walter. "But hurry, hurry!"

Ma Kettle's back was still turned. Walter slipped away and darted through crowds to the other side of the dock.

"Careful, careful!" he warned himself.

The bargee was his enemy too. He was on

the Master's side, paid by him to lure innocent lads to sea.

But the bargee was busy, laughing and joking with a seaman on the dock side. He wasn't even looking in Walter's direction.

Walter didn't hesitate. He climbed aboard and wriggled backwards into the piles of horse muck. He made himself a spy hole that he could breathe through and see the world. Then, buried in his warm, stinking hiding-place, he waited.

Every nerve in his body seemed to be shrieking, "Get me away from here!" But the barge wasn't moving. They were bound to be looking for him by now. Even though he was hidden in the horse manure Walter was frantic. "They will find me! I know they will!"

As Ma Kettle said, "Fisher lads don't escape that easy."

It felt like the whole world was out there searching just for him.

Then the barge shuddered beneath him.

"We're moving!" thought Walter.

He peeped through his spy hole, saw the dockside getting further away and the people on it shrinking. The barge didn't head for the cold, green waves of the open sea. It slid up river on the grey waters of the Humber. Soon Walter could see fields.

"We're out in the countryside!" he thought.

For the first time, he dared to hope.

It was so different from his journey down river. Then he had dozed on a bed of hay, in golden sunshine, full of daydreams about the sea.

"But you was greener than a cabbage then!" Walter reminded himself.

In the last weeks he'd had to grow up far too fast. He'd seen his friend drowned, been beaten and lashed with a rope's end, and spent ten days in jail.

"There's one thing come out of it, Walter," he told himself with a sad sigh. "At least now you know for certain – you and the sea ain't suited!"

We Thought We Had Lost You

Walter didn't mind the rich, rotten smell of horse manure.

"At least I'm safe in here," he thought.

Snug as a worm in its burrow.

Suddenly the barge stopped. Walter heard voices, footsteps on the barge. He could see

boots out of his spy hole, the sharp edge of a shovel. A farm worker had come on board to unload the muck!

"What do I do now?" thought Walter panicking.

If he stayed here that shovel could cut him in two. If he showed himself he would be caught and sent back to sea.

The bargee called out something. The boots stamped off. Walter gulped hard. He had to take the risk. He slithered out of his hiding place and dropped over the side into some tall **bulrushes**. He stayed there, up to his waist in water, hardly daring to breathe.

At last the barge floated off towards another farm. The farm worker's whistling faded away.

"Where am I?" wondered Walter.

He waded dripping up the bank. He looked around.

"I know where I am!" he thought joyfully. "I am nearly home!"

His own cottage was two fields away, just over that hill.

He trudged off, soggy with river water, plastered with muck and straw. He'd dreamed about coming home from sea a hero, with brand new boots, gold coins jingling in his pocket, and presents for everyone. He'd imagined how pleased they'd all be to see him.

"Ma and Pa won't want to know me now," he thought, miserably. "I runned away without telling them. And now I am come back in this wretched state."

He tried to wipe the horse manure out of his hair. But only smeared it over his face.

"Walter!"

It was Ma, hurrying up the track to meet him. Walter opened his mouth, tried to explain, "I'm sorry, Ma!" But Ma threw her arms around him, stinking and filthy as he was. She gave him a hug.

"Walter, son! We thought we had lost you!"

Later, Walter was sitting by the fire. He hadn't had time to wash yet, they'd made such a fuss of him. But when Pa came in he had some stern words: "You shouldn't have took off without telling us."

Ma said, "That Master! We wrote letters to him. We begged him to set you free. But he had a heart of stone! He said, 'I own your boy, body and soul, for the next ten years. I have the power of the Law on my side.' What an awful man!"

"Not everyone I met was awful," said Walter. "I made a friend called Alfred. He said he would stick by me."

Walter's eyes grew misty and sad. He was

remembering Alfred's cheeky grin. The way he'd never admit to being afraid.

"I should like to thank that Alfred," said Ma. "For being a friend to my boy,"

"You can't thank him, Ma ," said Walter. "I wish you could. He got drowned on our first day out."

Pa sighed. He patted Walter's shoulder. "You have had a hard time, son," he said. Then he asked, "Will that Master give you up? Or will he come looking for you?"

"I don't know," said Walter, looking

worried. What if the Master could hunt him down, even here. "I can't go back to sea," cried Walter desperately. "But if I stay here, he might find me."

"Your Ma and me have thought about that," said Pa in a calm voice. "There's a baker in the town. He is willing to take you on as his apprentice. To live with him and his family."

"I don't want to be apprenticed again!" said Walter.

"But he is a kind man, a good Master," said Ma. "We made sure of that. And you will see us every Sunday."

Walter thought about it. Hot ovens, the smell of fresh baking bread, plenty of pies to eat, and no fear of being caught by his old Master. Being a baker's boy sounded better then crow scaring. And far, far better than being a fisher lad.

"I will go to see this baker," Walter decided.

Pa stared at his son. He sounded so serious, so old for his age. He had only been away for three weeks but he had changed so much.

"Best scrub that horse muck off first, boy," grinned Pa. " I wouldn't want you baking *my* bread."

Walter said, "Good idea, Pa!" He gave Pa a big grin back.

Why did his smiling muscles seem so stiff? And then he realised. It was his first smile in ages. He gave Pa another big grin to make sure they were still working properly. Then went off to find a scrubbing brush.

Story Background

In Victorian times, many boys became fishing apprentices in ports like Grimsby. Some thought life at sea would be a great adventure. Some wanted to escape the terrible conditions in workhouses. They had no idea that life for a fishing apprentice or a deck hand could be even more terrible.

This painting shows the inside of a fishing smack in Victorian times. It is painted in a romantic style, and shows life at sea as ordered and safe. Was it like that for young apprentices?

Portrait of Thomas Cook (1808–1892), seated at his writing desk

Captain Thomas Cook, the famous sailor, was also a farm labourer's son who wanted to go to sea. He started off in small ships carrying coal and other goods and went on to sail around the world and make many famous voyages. Fortunately for him, life at sea turned out to be the way that Walter and Alfred dreamed it would be for them.

Although Walter Claridge is a fictional character, his story is based on the typical life and experiences of a Victorian fishing apprentice.

The historical evidence that the author used for building a story around this character came from four main areas:

◆ Fishing Registers
◆ Photographs
◆ Letters written by parents to newspapers
◆ Articles in newspapers

All these sources are available in public libraries, and you can find information on the internet. Try **http://www.grimsby webfind.com/sites/fishing/ boy_apprentices.htm** and **http://www.mariners-l.co.uk/ UKFisherman.html**

Photographs showing fishing apprentices are almost non-existent. This one shows two apprentices (back row second from right and bottom left).

An early photograph of fishermen taken in Grimsby. Note the two young fisher lads in the photo

Understandably, modern towns like the Grimsby of today are not proud of this part of their history. How important do you think it is that we know about the lives of boys like Walter and his friend Alfred?

Index

• •

Glossary

apprentice someone who is committed to an employer for a particular length of time to learn a craft

bargee a person in charge of a barge

bulrushes tall rushes growing in and around water

deck hand worker on a boat who carries out the orders of those in charge

first mate second in command on a boat

fishing smack single masted sailing boat used for fishing

guernseys thick knitted woollen jersey

indentures people who have legally agreed to be apprenticed

leads lumps of lead dropped into the water to test the depth

Master a trained person to whom someone might be apprenticed

oilskins outer garments which have been waterproofed with oil

Skipper captain of a vessel

trawl warp large wide-mouthed fishing net

undertow the current below the sea's surface